THE BIRDS' GIFT

A Ukrainian Easter Story

retold by Eric A. Kimmel
illustrated by Katya Krenina

Holiday House/New York

Library of Congress Cataloging-in-Publication Data
Kimmel, Eric A.
The birds' gift: a Ukrainian Easter story / retold by Eric A.
Kimmel; illustrated by Katya Krenina. — 1st ed.
p.   cm.
Summary: Villagers take in a flock of golden birds nearly frozen
by an early snow and are rewarded with beautifully decorated eggs
the next spring.
ISBN 0-8234-1384-5
[1. Easter eggs—Folklore.   2. Folklore—Ukraine.]   I. Krenina,
Katya, ill.   II. Title.
PZ8.1.K567Bk   1999
[398.2'09477'036]—dc21   97-50209   CIP   AC

To Katya,
who told me the story
E. A. K.

To Stefania Olege
and the wonderful bond
between grandparents and grandchildren
K. K.

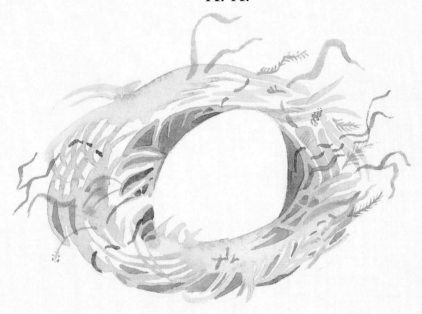

Grandfather Frost had come in the night, painting the windows with intricate patterns that looked like frozen flowers. Katrusya scratched the frost from the nearest pane. Snow covered the village as far as she could see. Suddenly she jumped. An eye stared back at her from the other side of the windowpane. Grandfather! How he loved to play tricks! Icicles hung from the ends of his long mustache. As he spoke, the white clouds of his breath mingled with smoke from his pipe.

"Come outside before the others wake up. We have a world of snow all to ourselves."

Katrusya dressed quickly. She buttoned up her coat and covered her head with a *hustka*, a colorful scarf that the women of the village tied over their ears. She pulled a pair of thick felt boots over her woolen socks and hurried out the door.

"I knew winter would be early this year. I felt it in my bones. The grain is hardly in the barn. Sunflowers are still standing in the garden, and here comes the snow," Grandfather said.

The snow nearly reached the top of Katrusya's boots as she and her grandfather walked through the silent village, all the way to the forest. Grandfather stopped beneath a birch tree to shake snow from his hat. Katrusya stuck out her tongue to catch the flakes falling from the sky.

Suddenly she stopped. "What's that?" Katrusya pointed to the foot of the tree. A fleck of gold shone like a buried coin through the snow.

Grandfather bent down. "It's a bird. A little golden bird."

Katrusya stared at the half-frozen creature cradled in her grandfather's mittens. The little bird peeped pitifully.

"How did it get here?" Katrusya asked.

"This happens when winter comes early," Grandfather explained. "Flocks of birds get caught in the snow and freeze. It is heartbreaking to see."

"Can't we do anything?" Katrusya asked.

"We can take the bird home and put it by the stove. But what good is saving one little bird when hundreds may be dying?"

"Let's look for them. Please, Grandfather! We must save the birds—as many as we can find!"

Katrusya tiptoed among the trees. *Peep! Peep! Peep!* She heard tiny voices chirping beneath the drifts. She brushed the snow aside. Underneath lay dozens of birds. Most were still alive, but so terribly frozen they could hardly open their beaks. Katrusya plucked birds from the snow, one after another.

Katrusya filled her coat. Her pockets bulged with birds. She tucked some inside each mitten and three into her scarf. Grandfather carried his share of birds, too. And still there were more.

"We'll take them home and come back for the rest," Grandfather said.

Katrusya and Grandfather arrived just as Mama was preparing breakfast. A big bowl of steaming kasha stood on the table. Katrusya opened her coat. A flock of tiny birds flew around the room.

"What is this?" cried Mama. "Where did these birds come from?"

"Oh, *Mamaniu,* we need help!" said Katrusya. "The birds are dying in the snow. Grandfather and I brought home as many as we could find, but there are still more out there."

"I'll help," said Katrusya's older sister, Lyuba, buttoning her coat.

"So will we!" said her brothers, Ivan and Danilo, setting aside their steaming bowls of buckwheat porridge. "We'll get the other boys to come, too."

"There will be more birds than can fit in one house. I'd better open the barn," said *Tato*, her father.

Katrusya and Grandfather returned to the forest. They did not go alone. News about the little birds spread through the village. Everyone came to help. They tucked birds inside their coats, hats, and mittens. They lined baskets with warm quilts and filled them with birds. They carried birds back to the village until all the houses and barns were full. And still there were more!

"Where can we put them?" Katrusya cried.

Father Roman, the priest, came running from the village.
"What is this I hear about a miracle of birds?" he asked.

"The birds need our help, Father!" Katrusya said. "There are so
many! We don't have room for them all. If they're left in the snow,
they will die."

"I know a place with lots of room," said Father Roman. "What
better shelter for God's creatures than God's own house? Bring
them to the church. There is no better deed than showing
kindness to others."

Everyone carried birds to the church until there were no more
to be found. The tiny creatures fluttered among the eaves like
flecks of living gold. They filled the church with their chirping.

Father Roman stretched out his arms. "Welcome, little birds!
Thank you for blessing us with your joyous song."

The snow stopped falling that evening, but the bitter weather continued for weeks. More snow fell. Columns of ice hung from the eaves of the houses. Trees in the forest cracked under the weight of ice and snow. They sounded like gunshots. It was the coldest winter in memory. Not even Granny Gurko could remember one like it.

Yet, strange to say, the winter did not seem as long or as dreary as it might have. The golden birds, perched in the eaves of every home, brought a bright note of spring. In church on Sunday they chirped and trilled as the choir sang hymns. They perched on Father Roman's shoulders as he preached the sermon.

"Listen to the birds," Father Roman told the congregation. "They worship God with every chirp, with every flutter of their wings. Would that human beings had such beautiful and perfect faith!"

One morning the birds behaved strangely. They gathered by the windows, flapping their wings, chirping wildly as they flung themselves against the glass panes.

Katrusya and Grandfather hurried to ask Father Roman's advice. They were not alone. Someone from every house was there. Each person had the same question. "What is wrong with the birds?"

"They want us to let them go," Father Roman explained.

"But winter is not over yet," Katrusya protested. She did not want her friends to leave.

"Trust the birds. They know what is best," the priest told her gently.

"When must we release them?" Grandfather asked.

"On Sunday, after church."

That Sunday Father Roman read the story of Creation, how God created the world in six days. While the birds chirped and flew about the windows, he spoke of a time to come, when lions would lie down with lambs and all creatures would live in peace. Katrusya listened to every word. She hoped that time would come soon, and that Grandmother and Grandfather—even old Granny Gurko—would live to see it.

Father Roman finished by saying, "Now we must show our love for our fellow creatures. It is time to set the birds free." He walked to the doors and threw them open wide. The birds flew outside in a fluttering golden stream. "*Idit z Bogom, malenki druzi! Go with God, little friends!*" Father Roman said.

The birds circled the church and perched in the snow-covered trees, calling to the others in the houses.

"Go home. Free the birds," said Father Roman.

Katrusya and her family hurried home. Together they counted to three. Then all at once, they threw open every door and window. Every house in the village did the same. A golden flock of yellow birds filled the sky. They circled over the snow-topped roofs, then flew away toward the forest, above the trees. Within minutes they were gone.

Katrusya found herself crying. She felt as if a piece of her heart had flown away. The tears froze on her cheeks.

"God will protect the birds," Grandfather murmured. "We will see them again. I can feel it in my bones."

The rest of winter passed slowly, like a great icicle melting drop by drop. Muddy patches appeared from beneath the snow. The sun emerged from behind the clouds. Crocuses pushed their heads above the melting ice. Spring had come at last.

And then it was Easter. Katrusya and Lyuba combed and braided each other's hair and tied it with bright ribbons. They put on new linen blouses, white as lilies, which they had woven, sewn, and embroidered themselves all through the long winter. Ivan and Danilo polished their boots until they gleamed like mirrors. *Tato* and Grandfather wore their finest shirts, beautifully embroidered with intricate patterns. Grandmother wore her gold earrings. Mother put on her necklace of coral beads.

As Katrusya stepped outside the house, she noticed something in the newly sprouted grass. "An egg!" she exclaimed. "An Easter egg!"

No one had ever seen an egg as beautiful as this. It was blue and gold, decorated with designs of birds flying over sheaves of wheat.

"Here's another!" cried Ivan.

"I found one, too!" Danilo echoed.

The children of the village hunted everywhere. They found more beautiful eggs, dozens of them, each decorated with a unique pattern. They gathered the eggs in baskets and brought them to the church.

"Where did these eggs come from?" they asked the priest.

Father Roman laughed. "Look up!"

They all raised their eyes. The trees in the forest, the church
dome, and the thatched roofs of the village were filled with birds.
The same golden birds they had sheltered throughout the long
winter.

"The birds have given us an Easter gift," Father Roman
explained.

"No two eggs are alike. Each one is different. Each is beautiful
and precious in its own way. So is every living creature in the eyes
of God."

Ever since that day, in memory of the birds' gift, people have made *pysanky*, the most beautiful Easter eggs of all.

They are a symbol of hope and life, of spring's triumph over winter, and of God's endless love for all creatures, great and small.

Author's Note

The art of decorating eggs—*pysanky*—is one of the oldest traditions of the Ukrainian people. Even before the coming of Christianity, the steppe people used eggs in their religious worship. The egg symbolized rebirth. The yolk represented the sun and the white, the moon. As a Christian symbol, the Easter egg represents the Resurrection of Christ, the triumph of life over death.

Pysanky are traditionally made by the women of the household after the rest of the family has gone to sleep. Only fertile eggs are used. Different blessings are asked for each *pysanka*, with the hope that the eggs will bring luck and good fortune to the people receiving them.

Designs are drawn on each egg with melted beeswax, using a metal stylus called a *kistka*. After each portion of the design is completed, the egg is dipped in one of several clay pots containing different colored dyes. The finished eggs are placed in a large bowl that is set in the oven. The melted wax is wiped off with a clean cloth.

Popular *pysanky* designs include birds, hearts, flowers, sheaves of wheat, spiders, ladders, and the sun, moon, and stars. Many different colors are used, with red being the most popular. Every egg carries a blessing, and each tells a story.